Traffic School

Carmel Reilly
Photographs by Lindsay Edwards

Contents

Meeting Our Coach

On Wednesday, I went to Traffic School
with some kids from my class.
This is a place where children can find out about
keeping safe while riding bicycles on the road.

When we got there,
a coach from the Traffic School
came to meet us.
She talked to us about
what we would be doing for the day.
Then, she took us to pick up our bikes,
helmets and **vests**.

Getting Ready to Ride

The coach showed us how to check that our bikes were safe for us to ride.

First, we had to see if the seats needed to be moved up or down.

Next, we checked that the tyres were full of air and the chains were on tightly.

Then, we tried our bells and brakes to check that they were working well.

The coach talked to us about what
we should wear when we are riding on the road.

She showed us how to put on yellow vests.
These help drivers to see us
when we are riding our bikes in **traffic**.

After that, the coach told us to put on our helmets.
She checked that they fitted well
and the straps were done up tightly.

Following the Road Signs

At last, we were ready to go!
We got on our bikes and followed our coach
onto one of the roads at the Traffic School.

The road had a white line down the middle.
The coach told us we had to keep
to the left side of that line.

She said we should ride slowly.
We mustn't get too close
to the bike in front of us.

Next, we practised riding across a **zebra crossing**.

As soon as we saw the zebra crossing ahead,
the coach told us to slow down.
She said we needed to be ready to stop
in case someone suddenly stepped out.

As we got closer, someone walked
onto the crossing.
But it was easy for us to stop
because we were not going quickly.

After that, we practised what to do
at a Stop sign.

We rode our bikes up to the Stop sign
and stopped.
We looked left and right to check for traffic.

The coach told us that we could only move on
if nothing was coming.

We waited while another bike rider went by.
When she had gone,
we checked again, then kept riding.

STOP

Doing Everything Right

The last thing we did was to ride around the Traffic School for five minutes. The coach stood and watched to see that we were doing everything right. She told us we had all done a great job of following the traffic signs.

We all liked going to Traffic School. We found out a lot about staying safe on the road. And it was fun, too!

Glossary

traffic (*noun*) cars and trucks moving along a road

vests (*noun*) tops with no sleeves, worn over other clothing

zebra crossing (*noun*) a part of the road painted with white lines for people to walk across